I0703407

Meet My Family of Cats

By Steven Williams

Meet My Family of Cats
Copyright © 2023 Steven Williams
All rights reserved. Printed in the United States of America.
No part of this book may be used or reproduced in any manner whatsoever without written permission except in the case of brief quotations embodied in critical articles and reviews. For information address Steven Williams, swilliamsjr87@yahoo.com.

ISBN 978-1962290807

Second Edition

For Parker,
whom I love eternally.

To my wonderful wife, Kerry,
who supports my every creation.

Hello! I'd like you to meet my family of cats.

There is...

Susan
The Vocal One

First up is Susan,
fluffy and grand,

Loving the spotlight,
you'll understand.

She folds back her ear,
with a touch of flair,

Jumps into boxes, or
climbs high in the air.

But her greatest joy,
you'll come to learn,

Is cuddling up,
it's love she'll return.

Ellie
The Hyper One

Ellie's a lively kitty,
full of pep and zip.

She sharpens her claws,
especially the tip.

Sneaks up on other cats,
just for a laugh.

Strong like a boxer,
perfecting her
choreograph.

Quick as a ninja,
she darts through the air.

And oh, how she
loves her catnip,
beyond compare!

Tedward

The Hungry One

Tedward's an orange tabby, fierce but divine.

With his very cute face, he's quite popular online.

Yet if he's ignored,
he'll meow and complain.

Demanding his dinner,
he's kind of a pain.

Once he gets food,
he's full and content.

Tedward's the cat where
love's time is well spent.

Janet
The Scary One

Janet's quite the kitty,
can give you a fright,

With other cats around,
she's not always polite.

She loves being solo,
with her person in sight,

Yet can be sweet, when
the mood is just right.

She'll bring in some grass,
a gift from her heart.

Just remember,
she's the queen—
that's her favorite part.

Abby
The Sweet One

Abby is sweet,
a true furry friend.

She bathes the other
cats, on her they depend.

Never in trouble,
not Abby, no way.

She drools just a bit,
but that's quite okay.

Cuddled in blankets,
she purrs without end.

With Abby around,
you've got a true friend.

Miyagi
The Chill One

Miyagi's the oldest,
resting his eye.

Awakening gently,
he lets out a large sigh.

Taking great care of
his teeth and his coat,

Day dreaming of pirates
and ships that will float.

And a samurai ready for action, sword in hand.

When night comes to call, it's relaxation he's planned.

These are my kitty cats, so dear and fun,
I hope you loved meeting each and every one.

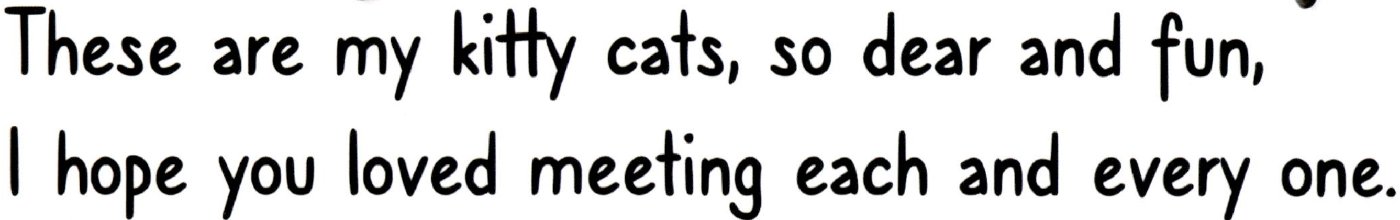

They're not perfect, this much is true,
But they love with all their hearts, through and through.

Each furry friend is more than just a pet,
In my heart, they stay, the best friends I've met!

About The Author

I've always considered our cats to be part of the family —each one with its own unique personality. One night, while sharing bedtime stories with my son, inspiration struck me. I thought, Why not create a children's book featuring our cats?

My goal was simple: to give my son a bedtime story that was not only fun but also held deeper meaning. What started as a playful idea soon became something much more—a cherished keepsake for him and a heartfelt tribute to the cats we love.

"Thank you for letting my family be a part of yours."

-Steven Williams

The Real Cats

All the cats featured in this book are real cats… with real attitudes. All their personality traits are true as well. From Ted whining to be fed and Janet sometimes being a scary kitty, to Abby simply being the best (I may have a favorite), every pretty kitty is as animated in real life as they are in this book.

Abby, Susan, and Janet

Tedward, Ellie, and Miyagi